Good-bye,
Funny
Dumpy-Lumpy

by BERNARD WABER

HOUGHTON MIFFLIN COMPANY, BOSTON, 1977

Library of Congress Cataloging in Publication Data

Waber, Bernard.
  Goodbye, funny dumpy-lumpy.

  SUMMARY: Five vignettes reveal how a mother, father,
and their three children negotiate common family problems.
  [1. Family life — Fiction]   I. Title.
PZ7.W113Go   [Fic]   76-14349
ISBN 0-395-24735-7

Contents

for
ANDREW

BENJAMIN

LISA

LORRAINE

RAFAEL

and

RICARDO

In the small village of Whitetip Corners
lived a mother, a father, and three children.
Monroe, the eldest of the children,
and Eudora, his younger sister,
were of school age.

Little Octavia, the third child, was still
too young for school.

"There are times when I think I do not
understand children," said Mother.
"Doesn't everybody?" said Father.

Everybody

"Good-bye," said Monroe, rushing off to school.

"Wear a jacket," said Mother.

"Wear a hat," said Father.

"But it's spring," said Monroe.

"Spring is a good time to catch cold," said Mother.

"It's the best time," said Father.

Monroe looked out the window.

"Everybody is outside without a jacket and a hat."

"I am not everybody's Mother," said Mother.

"I am not everybody's Father," said Father.

"Look!" said Monroe, "the sun is shining."

"Ah, but do you see robins?" said Father.

"Where are the robins?" asked Octavia.

"They are in a warm place," said Mother.

"Because they don't have hats," said Father.

"And they don't have jackets," said Mother.

"Who?" said Octavia.

"The robins," said Father.

"All right," said Monroe, "I will wear a hat."

"And a jacket," said Mother.

"And a jacket," said Monroe.

"But, I won't button up."

"He won't button up," said Mother.

"You will button up," said Father.

"Halfway," said Monroe.

"All right," said Father, "halfway."

"And Eudora, where is your schoolbag?" said Mother.

"They don't carry schoolbags anymore," said Eudora.

"They?" said Father.

"Who are they?" said Mother.

"Everybody," said Eudora.

"If everybody wore feathers, would you?" asked Mother.

"If everybody jumped into a river, would you?" asked Father.

"That's different," said Eudora.

Mother looked out the window.

"I see Jerome is carrying a schoolbag."

"Oh, Jerome," said Eudora.

"What's the matter with Jerome?" said Father.

"Nothing is the matter with Jerome," said Eudora.

"Then why did you just say 'oh, Jerome' the way
you just said 'oh, Jerome'?" said Mother.

"Because everybody knows how Jerome is," said Eudora.

"How is Jerome?" said Father.

"He is not like everybody," said Eudora.

"Did you ever?" said Mother.

"Monroe, your hat is on backwards," said Father.

"I know," said Monroe.

"He knows," said Mother.

"Everybody wears hats backwards," said Monroe.

"Again, everybody," said Mother.

"Who is everybody?" said Father.

"Just everybody," said Monroe.

Father looked out the window and exclaimed,
"Everybody is getting on the school bus!"
"Everybody?" said Monroe.
"Everybody?" said Eudora.
"That's a different kind of everybody," said Mother.
"That kind of everybody is all right," said Father.
"The bus is going to leave!" Octavia shouted.

"Hurry!" said Mother.

"Hurry!" said Father.

"How old is Great-Grandfather?" Eudora asked.
"He is one hundred years old," said Monroe.
"No, he is two hundred," said Octavia.

Great-Grandfather

One day, Great-Grandfather came for a visit.

Father helped him into the house.

Mother kissed him.

"How do you feel?" she asked.

"I feel old," said Great-Grandfather.

"Come, sit down," said Mother.

Great-Grandfather was helped to a chair.
Slowly, slowly, he sat down.
"Ah, this is good," said Great-Grandfather.
"Sitting is better than standing."

"Come, children," said Father. "Come and
kiss Great-Grandfather."
"What?" said Great-Grandfather.
"He is calling the children," said Mother.
"I want to see the children," said Great-Grandfather.

Monroe kissed Great-Grandfather.

"Ah, Joseph, what a big boy you are," said Great-Grandfather. "Do you help your mother and father?"

"This is not Joseph," said Father. "This is Monroe."

"Who?"

"Monroe," said Father.

"Ah, Monroe," said Great-Grandfather. "And this must be little Gloria."

"This is Eudora," said Father.

"Who?"

"Eudora," said Mother.

"Ah, Eudora. Of course," said Great-Grandfather. Eudora kissed Great-Grandfather.

"And here is Octavia," said Father.

"I don't want to kiss," said Octavia.

"Octavia," said Mother, "Great-Grandfather loves you."

"Who?" said Great-Grandfather.

Father looked at Octavia.

Octavia kissed the air around Great-Grandfather's cheek.

Great-Grandfather reached into his pocket.

"I have something for each of you," he said.

Great-Grandfather emptied his little change purse.

Out dropped several shiny coins.

"Here," said Great-Grandfather. "One for you, and
one for you, and one for you."

"Thank you," said Monroe, and Eudora, and Octavia.

"That was most generous of Great-Grandfather," said
Father. "Now, children, you can add those to your
piggy-bank."

"Can't we buy something this time?" said Monroe.

Mother looked at Father.

"All right," said Father.

"But not candy," said Mother.

Monroe, Eudora, and Octavia ran all the way to the
corner store.

"I want a balloon," Octavia told the storekeeper.

"I want one, too," said Eudora. "A red one."

"But I wanted red," said Octavia.

"I said red first," said Eudora. "Why don't you
get a yellow one?"

"I like red," said Octavia.

"You can't have red," said Eudora.

Octavia began to cry.

"All right," said Eudora, "we can both have red."

The storekeeper gave each of them a red balloon.

"And what will you have, sonny?" he asked Monroe.
"May I see that ball, please?" said Monroe.
The storekeeper gave Monroe the ball.

Monroe looked at the ball. He gave it back to
the storekeeper.
"May I see that little toy car, please?" said Monroe.
The storekeeper gave Monroe the little toy car.

Monroe looked at the little toy car. He gave it back
to the storekeeper.

"May I see that package of chewing gum?" said Monroe.

The storekeeper gave Monroe the package of chewing gum.

"Mother said, 'no candy,' " said Eudora.

"Chewing gum is not candy," said Monroe.

"Mother does not like us to have chewing gum, either,"
said Eudora.

"I'm going to tell," said Octavia.

Monroe gave the chewing gum back to the storekeeper.

"I didn't want chewing gum anyway," said Monroe.

"May I see that little toy airplane?"
The storekeeper gave Monroe the little toy airplane.
Monroe looked at the little toy airplane. He gave
it back to the storekeeper.

"Listen, sonny, you are going to have to make up your
   mind," said the storekeeper. "I haven't got all day."
"Uh . . ." said Monroe.
"Yes," said the storekeeper.
"I think I will uh . . ."
"Yes, yes," said the storekeeper.

"I'll have a balloon, too," said Monroe.

"What color?" said the storekeeper.

"Yellow," said Monroe.

The storekeeper gave Monroe a yellow balloon.

Monroe looked at it. He gave it back to the storekeeper.

"I think I'll take a blue one," said Monroe.

"Are you sure?" said the storekeeper.

"Make it a red one," said Monroe.

The storekeeper gave Monroe a red balloon.

"Thank you," said Monroe.

"Thank you," said the storekeeper.

"How will we know whose balloon is whose?" Eudora
asked, on the way home.

Just then, her balloon went . . . pop!

Monroe and Octavia laughed.

"Now, you won't have to worry about it," said Monroe.

"Monroe, will you let me play with your balloon?" she asked.

"Maybe," said Monroe.

"Will you let me play with your balloon?" she asked
Octavia.

"No," said Octavia, "I don't want it to get broken."

Just as she said "broken," her balloon went . . . pop!

Octavia began to cry.

Octavia came into the house crying.

"Shush!" said Mother. "Great-Grandfather has just gone up to bed."

"Already!" said Monroe. "Does Great-Grandfather go to bed even before Octavia?"

"I thought when you are old, you can stay up as long as you wish," said Eudora.

"Shush!" said Father. "Now children, go upstairs and say goodnight to Great-Grandfather."

The children went upstairs.
Great-Grandfather looked very small in the big bed.
"We came to say goodnight," said Monroe.
Great-Grandfather opened his eyes.
"Water," said Great-Grandfather.

"Here, Great-Grandfather," said Monroe. "Here is
your glass of water."

Great-Grandfather opened his eyes again.

"Thank you," he said. "Put it on the table."

Monroe put the glass of water on the table.

Then, Great-Grandfather did something surprising.

He put his hand to his mouth, took something out, and
put it into the water.

The children gasped.

"Teeth!" Eudora exclaimed. "Great-Grandfather put his
teeth into the water."

"They are false teeth," said Monroe.

"Great-Grandfather, can you take your tongue out, too?"
said Octavia.

"Shush!" said Monroe.

"He is sleeping," said Eudora.

"He is sleeping very quietly," said Monroe.

"Is he breathing?" asked Eudora.

"I'm not sure," said Monroe.

"Maybe he is dead," said Octavia.

"Shush!" said Monroe.

"I am frightened," said Octavia.

Just then, Great-Grandfather made a loud snoring sound,
The children jumped back.

They raced downstairs.

"Mother! Father!" they cried out. "Great-Grandfather put his teeth into the glass of water!"

"Shush" said Mother.

"Shush!" said Father.

"Look what I found!" said Octavia.
"The rickety leg!" Mother exclaimed.
"It must have dropped off when they took
the old sofa away."

Good-bye, Funny Dumpy-Lumpy

The old sofa was really old, and it was funny dumpy-lumpy
in the middle.
"If only these pillows would lie flat," Mother
often sighed.
One of the sofa legs was rickety, and the children liked
rocking back and forth on it, as if on a swing.

Once, Father tried gluing the leg tight.
"There!" said Father, when he was finished, "it's as
tight as a drum. I defy anyone to try rocking it now."
Everyone sat on the sofa at once.
It was tight all right. It didn't rock one bit.

But then one day, Cousin Harriet, and Duane,
her new husband, came for a visit.
Suddenly, just as Father was offering grape soda, there
was a noise like a rusty gate slamming, and the sofa
collapsed. Cousin Harriet fell on top of Duane. And Duane
spilled grape soda all over his clean white suit.

"It's ruined!" Mother cried, scrubbing Duane's suit with a damp cloth.

"Oh, this old suit," said Duane. "I never cared for it much anyway. The lapels are far too wide."

Father lent Duane a suit. And he put a telephone
book under the corner of the sofa.
After a while, everyone settled back and laughed about
how funny it was the way the sofa collapsed.

But after Cousin Harriet and Duane said goodnight,
Mother burst into tears.
"It was humiliating!" she cried.
"We'll have to do something about that old sofa,"
said Father.

But the Family really liked the old sofa.
Father liked snoozing on it after dinner.
And Mother did all of her letter writing on the
old sofa. She made herself comfortable, took out
her pen, and wrote and wrote and wrote.

The children
often hunted for buried treasure
in the old sofa.
They would reach deep down into the warm, dark, secret
places of the sofa, and feel for things.
Once Monroe found three coins and a baseball picture-card.
And Eudora found a link bracelet.
"Oh, I've been looking everywhere for that bracelet,"
said Mother.
And once, when Octavia was ill for several days,
Mother bedded her down on the old sofa.
"Just so you won't feel lonely upstairs, honey,"
said Mother.

One day, Mother said, "I was in the department
store today."
"Yes," said Father.
"And I saw the most beautiful sofa."
"Yes," said Father.
"It's the most perfect shade of green."
"Yes," said Father.
"And it's not too terribly expensive."
"Yes," said Father.
"And . . ."
"And you want to buy it."
"Yes," said Mother.

The next day, Mother, Father, and the children
went down to the department store.
"See," said Mother, pointing to the sofa,
"isn't it beautiful!"
"I like it," said Father.

"Why don't you try sitting on it," said the salesman.

Father sat on the sofa.

"Mmmmmmmmm," said Father, "no lumps. I like it very much." And so, Mother and Father bought the sofa.

The family had to wait six weeks for the new sofa. During that time, Father seemed to want to snooze on the old sofa more often than ever.

And Mother seemed to be writing letters more often than ever.

And the children seemed eager to rock, bounce, and search for buried treasure more often than ever.

At last, one afternoon, the new sofa arrived.
"Oh, they're taking out the old sofa!" Mother
called sadly.
"But you knew they would," said Father.

Everyone rushed outside as the old sofa was carried
onto the moving van.
And they looked one last look as it sat all alone,
seeming to sulk, in the dark insides of the huge van.

"I feel almost as if I want to wave good-bye,"
 said Mother, as the van pulled away.
"Oh, let's!" said Eudora. "Let's wave good-bye!"
"Good-bye!" Eudora called out.
"Good-bye, rickety leg!" called Monroe.
"Good-bye, funny dumpy-lumpy!" called Octavia.
"Good-bye, good-bye, dear old sofa!" called Mother.

"Well, no need to feel sad," said Father. "Now we
have a beautiful new sofa. Let's have a look at it."
The children looked suspiciously at the bright colored
stranger in the living room.
"Come, come!" said Father. "Isn't anyone going to sit
on it? It's meant to be sat upon, you know."

Everyone sat stiffly on the new sofa.

"It is nice, isn't it," said Mother.

"Well, isn't it?" said Mother.

"Yes," said Monroe.

"Yes," said Eudora.

"Mother, how long will it take for the new sofa
to grow lumps?" asked Octavia.

Mother smiled.

"A long, long time," she answered.

"Aunt Effie is crying," said Monroe.
"I never saw a schoolteacher cry," said Eudora.
"She cries the same way we do," said Octavia.

The Picnic

It was Sunday.
The children were looking out the window.
They were looking for Aunt Effie and Uncle Wally.
Soon, a motor car rumbled up the driveway.
"They are here!" cried Monroe.
The children ran outside.
Aunt Effie kissed them.
Uncle Wally put Monroe
on his shoulders, and swept
Eudora and Octavia
up in each of his arms.
"Uncle Wally! Uncle Wally!
May I sit in your car?"
cried Monroe.
"Of course,"
said Uncle Wally.

Mother and Father came out.

"What a lovely day for a picnic!" said Aunt Effie.

"Glorious!" said Mother.

"Do I smell rhubarb pie?" said Uncle Wally.

"Can you smell it out here?" Mother laughed.

"I can smell rhubarb pie a mile away," said Uncle Wally.

Honk! Honk!

"Monroe! Stop honking the horn!" Father called out.

Honk! Honk!

"Monroe, did you hear me!" Father called again.

"You would think they had never seen a car," said Mother.

"We are waiting for you," Monroe cried out.

"I suppose we should be on our way," said Mother,

"and have full advantage of this beautiful day."

Soon, everyone was in the car, driving to the lake.

At the lake, they chose to picnic under a huge, shady tree.
And while Mother, Father, and Aunt Effie began to prepare
the picnic table, Uncle Wally played games with
the children.
First, they played catch with the ball Uncle Wally
had brought for them.

After that, they played tag, had a potato sack race,
and flew the kites Uncle Wally had made especially for
the children. Each kite had a name printed on it:
MONROE, EUDORA, OCTAVIA.
The children shrieked gleefully as they watched the
kites bob in the wind.
"Mine is highest!" Monroe cried out.
"No, mine is!" Eudora shouted back.
"Why won't mine go up?" wept Octavia.
Uncle Wally helped Octavia with her kite.
He gave it more line, and soon her kite was as high
as the others.

"Lunch is ready," said Mother.

Uncle Wally helped bring down the kites.

Soon everyone was seated at the picnic table.

They had a delicious lunch of tuna and egg salad sandwiches, rhubarb pie, watermelon, and wine for the grown-ups.

"Have some more wine," said Uncle Wally.

"No, thank you," said Father.

"Not for me, either," said Mother. "Wine makes me sleepy, and I'm having too good a time to want to be sleepy."

"Surely, we have all had enough wine," said Aunt Effie.

"Well, I'll just have another glass," said Uncle Wally.

Aunt Effie looked at Uncle Wally.

"I think I will go for a walk," said Aunt Effie.

"I'll come with you," said Eudora.

Eudora and Aunt Effie went for their walk.
"Tell me about when you were a schoolteacher,"
   said Eudora.
"That was a long time ago," said Aunt Effie.
"Before you married Uncle Wally?"
"Let's look at the flowers," said Aunt Effie.
"Tell me about it," said Eudora.
"What shall I tell you?"
"What did you like to do most, when you were a
   schoolteacher?"

"I liked reading stories."

"I like stories, too," said Eudora.

"I liked sitting at my desk, looking into the faces
   of my students. I liked discovering how best to help
   each of them learn."

"Did you have favorites?"

"I hope not," said Aunt Effie.

"I wish I had been in your class," said Eudora. "I
   would tell all of the children that you were my aunt."

"Eudora, you wouldn't!"

"I would," said Eudora. "I really would. And I would
   sit up front, right at your desk. And I would help
   you to erase the blackboard. And I would wait for you
   after school so we could walk home together. And everyone
   would say: There goes Eudora. She is walking with her
   aunt, the schoolteacher."

"Oh, Eudora!"

"Aunt Effie, I wish you were teaching school now.
   Don't you miss teaching?"

"Sometimes," said Aunt Effie.

"When I grow up, I am going to teach school, too,"
   said Eudora.

'You will make a fine teacher," said Aunt Effie.

"And I will never stop teaching," said Eudora. 'Never!"

"Perhaps we should go back now," said Aunt Effie.

Eudora and Aunt Effie walked back to the picnic.

They saw Father and Uncle Wally.

Uncle Wally's clothes were wet.

"What happened?" said Aunt Effie.

"He became dizzy," Father answered. "He fell in the lake."

"Perhaps he had a bit too much sun," said Mother.

"Or too much wine," said Aunt Effie.

"I want to lie down," said Uncle Wally.

"We are all tired," said Mother. "It's been a full day."

Father helped Uncle Wally into the car.
Suddenly, Aunt Effie began to cry.
Mother held her.
The children looked on in astonishment.
Octavia began to giggle.
"Stop that!" said Eudora.

Father came back.
"Come children," he said. "Let's gather everything together."
Soon they were in the car again.
Everyone was quiet as Father drove all the way home.

"We have a problem," said Mother.
"What is the problem?" said Father.
"We have three children."
"I know," said Father.
"But we only have two laps," said Mother.

The Outdoor Concert

"This is a good spot," said Father. "It's close
to the bandstand."
Father spread a blanket.

Everyone sat down.

"I want to sit next to Mother," said Octavia.

"I was here first," said Eudora. You can sit
next to Father."

"I am sitting next to Father," said Monroe.

"I have nobody to sit next to," cried Octavia.

"You are sitting next to me," said Eudora.

"You know what I mean," said Octavia.

"Here," said Mother, "you can sit between us."

Mother and Father made room in the middle for Octavia.

"Is everyone comfortable?" asked Father.

"I don't have enough blanket," said Eudora. "I am sitting on the grass."

"Would everyone please move over just a bit?" said Father. Everyone moved over.

"But, now, I don't have enough blanket," said Monroe.

"How about if we all move toward the middle," said Father. Everyone moved toward the middle.

"I'm being scrunched!" cried Octavia.

"Octavia, would you like to sit on my lap?" asked Mother.

"Yes," said Octavia.

Octavia climbed onto Mother's lap.

"I would like to sit on your lap," said Eudora.

"I was here first," said Octavia.

"Can we take turns?" said Eudora.

"No," said Octavia.

"Yes," said Mother.

"When will it be my turn?" asked Eudora.

"Why don't you sit on Father's lap," said Octavia.

"I am going to sit on Father's lap," said Monroe.

Monroe climbed onto Father's lap.

"I don't have a lap to sit on," wept Eudora.

"But we only have two laps," said Mother.

"We'll take turns," said Monroe. "I'll sit on Father's lap for a while, and then you can sit on Father's lap."

"But, I want to sit on Mother's lap," said Eudora.

"You can't," said Octavia.

"We can take turns," said Eudora.

"It's getting dark," said Mother. "The stars are beginning to shine. And, oh, look at the moon! Isn't it lovely!"

"Can't we take turns?" said Eudora.

"No," said Octavia.

"Yes," said Mother.

"The musicians are arriving," said Father. "Look
  at the shiny instruments!"
"Aren't they beautiful!" said Mother.
"May I go and watch the musicians?" asked Monroe.
"Yes," said Father. "But come back before the music begins."
"May I go with Monroe?" asked Eudora.
"I want to go, too," said Octavia.
"All right," said Father.
"But please stay together."

The children ran off.
"Now we have empty laps,"
said Mother.
"What a waste!" said Father.

The orchestra began to tune up.
The children ran back to Mother and Father.
Monroe climbed onto Father's lap.
Eudora and Octavia looked at Mother's lap.
"Eudora, you can sit on Mother's lap," said Octavia.
"Oh, thank you," said Eudora.
"We have considerate children," said Mother.
"We most certainly have," said Father.
"But only for a while, Eudora," said Octavia.

Tap! Tap! Tap!

The orchestra leader raised his baton.

Suddenly, there was a drum beat.

"That's the bass drum," said Monroe.

"How do you know?" asked Father.

"Because I know," said Monroe.

Now, the horns were playing.

"Isn't it lovely!" said Mother.

"Shush!" said someone nearby.

"We came to hear music."

"Sorry," Mother whispered.

Everyone sat quietly.

A warm, gentle wind arrived.

The trees began to sway, it seemed,

in time with the music.

And the stars began to twinkle, it seemed,

in time with the music.

And somewhere in the dark, a chirping cricket

decided to join the orchestra.

And the moon sat low, listening.

Octavia forgot all about Mother's lap.

When the concert was over, everyone applauded.

The conductor bowed deeply.

After that, the conductor made an announcement.

"Ladies and gentlemen!" he said, "we shall now have dancing."

The orchestra began to play dance music.

"Time to go home," said Mother.

"But aren't you going to dance!" cried Octavia.

"Oh, no," said Mother. "It's much past your bedtime. Besides," she laughed, "we haven't danced in years."

"Oh, you must dance!" Eudora exclaimed. "Just one dance?"

"Please?" said Octavia.

"Please?" said Monroe.

"Please?" said Father.

Mother looked at Father.

"You really want to dance?" said Mother.

"Yes," said Father.

"All right," Mother smiled. "Octavia, will you please hold on to my purse while we dance?"

"May I hold it?" said Eudora.

"She asked me," said Octavia.

"We can take turns," said Eudora.

"No," said Octavia.

"Now, now," said Father.

"All right," said Eudora, "you can hold it."

Mother and Father began to dance.
The children watched.
"Isn't Mother pretty!" said Eudora.
"Yes," said Monroe.
"Yes," said Octavia.